Slippery Willie's Stupid, Ugly Shoes

By Larry Peterson

Kravitz & Sons

Kravitz and Sons LLC
204 E Arlington Blvd. Suite B
Greenville, NC 27858

Published by Kravitz and Sons LLC.
ISBN: 979-8-89639-508-9(sc)
ISBN: 979-8-89639-509-6(e)

Library of Congress Control Number: 2025919033

Because of the dynamic nature of the Internet, any web addresses or links contained in this book may have changed since publication and may no longer be valid. The views expressed in this work are solely those of the author and do not necessarily reflect the views of the publisher, and the publisher hereby disclaims any responsibility for them.

Dedicated to all kids who think they are "different".
It does not matter...
How tall or short you are,
How big your nose is,
How fast you can run,
How high you can jump,
If you can see or not,
Hear or not,
Or even be wheelchair bound.
You are all God's special individual creations and
God "don't make no junk".

Slippery Willie's
Stupid, Ugly Shoes

Willie Wiggles was like most of the other kids in his class except for one thing. He had slippery feet. They were so slippery that Willie just slipped, slid, and spun all over the place. Even when Willie had his shoes on the slipperiness would slip out and he would still slip, slide, and spin. No one knew why Willie had slippery feet. Not even the smartest doctors could figure it out. Willie just had the slipperiest feet in the whole world and that was all there was to it.

Willie could not ride a bike because his feet would slip off the pedals. He could not climb a tree because his feet slipped off the branches. If he tried to run he would start spinning around and around until his feet slipped right off the ground.

Why sometimes his shoes and socks would slide right off his feet even when he was just sitting at his desk in school. Poor Willie. He just slipped, slid, and spun up, down, over, across, forwards, backwards, and sideways too. As you can imagine, Willie hated having slippery feet. However, there was one thing that Willie hated more.

Special new shoes had been made for him. They were going to stop him from slipping and sliding and spinning. Willie thought that they were the stupidest, ugliest, dumbest shoes he had ever seen anywhere. He just knew that if he wore them everyone would laugh and make fun of him. His mom and dad tried to convince him that he should not worry about what other people might think or say. But Willie did not care. He just hated his stupid, ugly, dumb shoes and that was all there was to it.

The morning came when Willie was to wear his stupid, ugly, dumb shoes for the first time. He was just slipping and sliding and spinning around the kitchen in his bare feet when his mom came in and said, "C'mon Willie, time to put on your new shoes. No more slipping and sliding for you."

"I don't want to wear them", he said as he slid up the wall.

"Please Willie", mom said. "You just have to try them. They will help you."

"I hate those shoes! I hate them! They are stupid, ugly, and dumb and everyone will laugh!"

Mom tried to be patient. "C'mon now, Willie. If you wear them you'll be able to ride your bike, or climb a tree and run and jump just like all the other kids."

"I don't care! I don't care! I hate them!"

Willie's mom tried to grab Willie so she could put the stupid, ugly, dumb shoes on his feet. But Willie slipped away from her and slid across the room. "Can't catch me", he said. "Can't catch me."

"We'll see about that", Willie's mom said laughing.

Willie's mom went to the closet and got out the large butterfly net. She started chasing after Willie. Willie slid around the kitchen table as his mom chased after him.

He slid up a wall and back down and just as he was about to slide up the stairs she flung the net over him. "Gotcha", she said laughing.

As Willie tried to get away mom caught him with the net. Then she put the stupid, ugly, dumb shoes on Willie's feet and locked them on with a big red key. Willie tried to get them off but he couldn't. So off to school he went mumbling and grumbling about his new shoes. He did not even realize he was just walking and not slipping and sliding.

When Willie walked into his classroom all the kids turned and looked at his new shoes. They all started laughing. The teacher asked, "What is so funny, children?"

"Look at Willie's shoes", said Christina. "They are the stupidest, ugliest, dumbest shoes anywhere."

"Let me see your shoes Willie", the teacher said.

Willie frowned and slowly held up his foot. The teacher looked, her eyes opened wide, and suddenly she started to laugh. "Why Willie", she said. "Those are uh-well-well, I guess they are the stupidest, ugliest, dumbest shoes I have ever seen." She began laughing so hard she fell down on the floor.

When the other kids saw this they too began laughing so hard that they were rolling around on the floor. The principal heard all of the noise and came in. When he saw Willie's shoes he laughed so hard that he knocked over a desk.

Willie could not believe what he was seeing. So he told the teacher that he was going home. She was laughing so hard she never heard him.

As Willie walked down the hallway kids and teachers in other classrooms saw him go by. By the time Willie left the school everyone inside was laughing louder and harder than they had ever laughed before.

As Willie walked away from the school he turned and looked back. The building was smiling. "Oh no", he said, "Even the building is laughing at these stupid, ugly, dumb shoes."

As Willie walked home strange things began to happen. Cars and trucks banged into each other because drivers were so busy laughing at Willie's shoes that they forgot to look where they were going.

A big blue bus went by rocking back and forth as all the passengers inside rolled around the aisle laughing.

Cats and dogs were laughing. Birds fell out of trees laughing. Even the quacks from the ducks at the pond turned into laughter.

Willie looked up and saw a big jumbo jet flying around in circles with its wings tipping back and forth as the people inside rolled around laughing.

Even people who had not seen Willie's shoes were laughing because they heard other people laughing.

Willie was sure that the entire world had gone crazy because of his stupid, ugly, dumb shoes.

When Willie walked up to his house his mom was outside. She too was laughing. "Oh no!", he screamed. "Not you too!"

Willie's mom looked at her boy. Then she said, "You were right Willie. Those are the stupidest, ugliest, dumbest shoes I have ever seen."

"Get them off me mom! Get them off me! Hurry!"

"Sorry Willie, I lost the key. Too bad."

"Please mom, get them off, these shoes made everyone go crazy! Get them off!"

"Okay Willie, okay. C'mon, get up. We'll find the key."

Willie slowly opened his eyes. He was in bed and his mom was sitting beside him. She saw this strange look on his face. "What's wrong Willie?" she asked.

Willie hollered, "The whole world is laughing at my stupid, ugly, dumb shoes and so are you!"

Willie's mom put her arm around her boy. "Oh Willie. You have been worrying so much about what people might say about your new shoes that you made yourself have a bad dream. That's all. No one was laughing at your shoes. You haven't even worn them yet."

Willie got dressed and put on his special shoes. He felt ridiculous. But to his surprise, when he got to school no one laughed. In fact, the other kids thought they were the neatest shoes they had ever seen. They all wanted to know where they could get shoes like that.

That afternoon when Willie got home he went up to his room. He took off his special shoes, smiled, and began slipping and sliding and spinning all over the place.

9 798889 639508 9